A DOG'S TALE

ISBN 1-58961-102-0

Published by PageFree Publishing, Inc.
8175 Creekside Drive
Portage, Michigan 49024
269-321-5030
www.pagefreepublishing.com

A DOG'S TALE

A story of the rescue of a dying dog and his Friendship with a lonely man.

Iris Revesz Rodak

For Joe, the dog everyone loves!

For Lee and Dawn

A special thanks for assistance in editing to Walter and Dorothy Martini and Lorn Shourd, Bobby and Kathy Mckee.

The man smelled different and he staggered when he walked. He had been gone all afternoon. I had not had anything to eat. I was starving! He started yelling at me! I had an accident some time earlier. I could not help it! I could not get out the door. The man yelled and swore at me. He swung his leg and the toe of his heavy boot struck me in the hip. I yelped, loud, it really hurt! It rolled me clear across the kitchen floor. I would feel that pain in my hip for months. In my older years I would get arthritis there. The man went to the closet and got out the long black pipe with the wooden handle. I started to shake! Somehow, I knew this was danger for me. The man grabbed my neck and shoved me out the door into the cold. He pointed the black pipe at me. I ran! I heard a loud boom and the snow flew up behind me. I kept on running! I did not look back! I would remember the sound of that booming black pipe all my life. I would tremble in fear whenever I saw one or heard that terrible sound! I would always be known as a gun shy dog and I was. My mother had warned me of many dangers. She told me about cars and roads, black pipes and people who had the acidy smell of anger about them.

The man had been good to me at first. He had been good to my mother too. Then she had done something that made the man yell and she was gone. I never saw her again. I cried all night when she disappeared. The man yelled at me and told me to shut up. I missed my mother but I learned to take care of myself as best I could. Teaching yourself is hard but I was smart and had a patient, gentle nature. For some time the man and I got along well. We even went for walks together.

Then he would go away for an afternoon. When he came home he smelled bad and was mean to me. He forgot to feed me or put water in my dish.

I was too young to care for myself. Now, I was running through the snow. It was freezing! It was getting dark! I was in a panic! I was just running as fast as I could not even caring where I was going. I just wanted to get away from the man who kicked me and shot at me.

I ran until I could not breathe. The cold air hurt my lungs! I had to stop! I was by a road. I remembered what my mother had said about cars and what happened if one hit you. I would not go on the road. I was standing in snow up to my belly. I was shivering, hard. I could not stop! I could feel myself start to freeze. My feet got colder and colder. My muscles started to hurt. I had been out in the wind and cold for a very long time. I began to feel light-headed and saw strange things. My mother's face swam before my eyes. I felt so tired. I just wanted to lie down and sleep!

Just as I was about to give up and accept my fate I noticed a little truck slowly coming down the road. The snow pelted its headlights. I knew that this was the only chance for me to survive. I tried to move toward the road. I was so cold I had trouble standing! The little truck pulled slowly to a stop on the far side of the road. A man in a dark jacket and cap got out. He shielded his eyes from the snow, peering at me. He was not sure what I was or if I was really there at all. The man crossed the snowy road, clambered through the ditch and came to me. He had kind eyes! He reached down and lifted me up. He carried me back and put me on the front seat of the little truck. He got in and put the heater on full blast. Never had warm air felt so good! I was saved!

The man talked to me, telling me not to worry.

"Everything is going to be all right," he said. I was so glad to hear his voice. It had the sound of caring in it.

I looked out the window of the little truck. The snow was falling faster and faster. The wind was whipping the snow sideways in big clouds of white. The spot where I had sat could not be seen now. If the man had come along just five minutes later he would never have been able to see me sitting by the side of the road! I would have sat there just waiting to be rescued. I would have died! The man put the little truck in gear and eased it out onto the highway. It was hard for him to drive. The road was slippery. It was hard to see because of the thick snow. The man said we were lucky because we did not have very far to go.

Soon we stopped. The man said this was his house. " It is little, but it is warm," he said. It was a tiny house with a small covered porch. It had a big window with a light shining in it. The light in the window looked warm and welcoming.

The man picked me up off of the seat and carried me into the house. He put me down on the couch. I was shaking so hard I could not stand. I could not stop my teeth from clicking together! The man hurried down the hall. Soon I could hear water running. The man came back, scooped me up off of the couch, and carried me down the hall. He put me in the tub which was full of warm water. It was heaven! The man sat on the edge of the tub and talked softly to me. "You will be all right," he said, "I will make sure of that."

When I was a little warmer
the man lifted me out of the
tub. He dried me with a big
towel. He rubbed me until I
was warm and dry. "You need
something to eat, "he said.
We went into the tiny kitchen
and he found some leftover
sausages. He cut them up in
little pieces and put them in a
bowl for me. They were
wonderful! I ate them all! My
hip still hurt like blazes but I
was warm at last. I was full
of delicious sausages.

I was happy! The man got an old quilt. He spread it on the floor of the living room. I curled up on it. I slept the sleep of the rescued. I had wonderful dreams.

The next morning the man took me out for a short walk. It was still bitterly cold so we did not go far. The man said, "Do your business." I did!

The man laughed and said that I was a good dog.

The man put me in the front seat of the little truck and we went to town. First, he went to a store and bought me a new dish and some special food. He loaded the food in the truck and then walked across the street. He went in a door and I could see him talking to a lady.

She kept shaking her head back and forth. Then she handed the man something. The man came out and got in

the truck. He said he guessed
we belonged to each other
now. He had a collar with a
little tag on it. He said we
should pick a name for me. He
said, "How about Joe, it's an
easy name to remember." I
liked that! My new name was
Joe. I had a tag with a number
on it. I had a new dish and
special food. I had an old quilt
to sleep on. Most importantly
I had a new friend and we
belonged to each other. The
man said he did not want a

dog. They are too much trouble. I did not want a man. They are too much trouble. But, now we had each other anyway!

Iris Revesz Rodak

The man started the truck and we went home. When we got to the man's home he carried the new dish and the special food into the kitchen. I followed him right inside. I guessed it was my house too.

I slept on the old quilt again that night. The man spent the evening watching TV. He talked softly to me as he stroked my head. I felt so warm and safe. Sometimes the man told himself funny stories and laughed out loud. He said he was a fireman and the next day he had to go to work. He told me that he would call a special friend to come visit me so I would not be lonely or have any accidents in the house. I was glad.

I knew what happened if you had an accident. Boom!

The next morning the man was up and dressed before it

got light outside. I heard a knock on the door. I did not bark! I was not sure yet if this was my job at this house. Should I warn the man if someone came? I did not want to make him angry at the noise of my warning bark. I'd wait and see what happened. He opened the door. A lady with a big smile stepped in. The man said, "How do you like my new buddy?" The lady came over to me and let me smell her hand. She did not stick her face in mine or start petting me right away. She let me decide if I liked her. She was very gentle like the man. I liked her! The man put on his coat and cap. He patted me on the head, went out the door and was off to work. The lady asked me if I wanted some breakfast. I went and sat by my new dish. "You are a smart little guy," she said. She gave me some of the special food and some clean water. Later, she took me outside for a walk. I was glad; I did not want to have an accident. We went for short little walks using a new leash she had brought with her.

The lady and I spent the day going for walks and watching TV. We watched the Animal Planet Channel.

She especially liked the Emergency Vets show. She laughed and said, "Joe, you and I will be friends and watch dog TV together." It sounded like a good idea to me.

The next day the man was back from work. He and I spent the first of many days together. Everywhere he went he took me with him in his little truck. I made lots of new friends. I met the man's friend Guy; Dawn the dog groomer who gave me a haircut, and Dr. Almus. He gave me a shot! Everyone admired me and how well behaved I was. I knew just what to do when we visited people. Never jump up on them. Never dig holes in their yards. Do not growl or bite. Most of the people liked me. They said they wished they had a dog just like me. The man said he understood, he thought I was pretty special too. When we left after a visit he said, "Joe, you are the dog everyone loves."

We fell into a routine. When the man was at work the lady came to stay. When the man was home the lady went away. The lady and I became good friends but I really loved the man the most. He had saved me. On the days the man was home I missed the lady and when the lady was with me I missed the man. I wanted them both with me all the time. I wanted a family.

Winter turned into spring, and then spring turned into summer. Time went by and the years passed pleasantly. The man lived on the shore of Lake Michigan. We often went to the beach. We walked for miles and miles on the sand. In the summer I chased seagulls. I never managed to catch one. They were noisy and messy. They could fly really fast. The lady brought me a rope toy. The man would throw it out into the lake. I chased after it! I learned to swim really well playing this game of fetch. I was fast and sleek. Sometimes the man and I met other people walking on the beach. They always admired me and asked the man what kind of dog I was. "Why, he's the best, that is what kind of dog he is," the man always said. I guess I was what was called a mix. Sometimes we met other walkers who had their dogs with them. The

man let me run to them and
sniff a hello. I never met a
mean dog at the beach. They
all seemed just as happy as I
was to be there. The beach
on a warm summer day was a
pure joy.

One day the man came
home from work early. He
asked the lady to stay for a
while as he needed to talk
with her. She made fresh
coffee and poured two cups.
She got me fresh water. She

and the man sat at the table to drink their coffee while I lay at the man's feet. Sometimes I appear to be sleeping when I am really listening. It is a trick most dogs can do, sort of like a car idling. I listened and heard some new words. The man talked to the lady about retiring, a new farm and marriage. He said the most important word, family!

Later that day the man and

the lady put me in the little truck. We drove out in the country. We went down a narrow road, turned up a dirt driveway and saw a small house on a hill. There were also a big barn and a small shed. There were pine trees all around. We got out of the truck and looked all around the yard. I could smell wonderful exciting smells wafting on the breeze and trailing through the overgrown grass. The scent of rabbits mixed with the scent of squirrels mixed with the scent of birds. It was so heady it made me dizzy. I ran with my head down, nose to the ground, just gulping up the delicious odors. I knew this was the place for me!

The man and the lady got married. They began working on the farm. They painted the barn, fixed up the little house and mowed the long grass. They planted a garden. They planted fruit trees. There was not a spot on the small farm that the man did not work at improving. It was a tiny farm but it had plenty of room for me to run and chase rabbits. The man took breaks from his chores every day and took me to the beach or for a walk in the woods. Often we found wild turkeys eating the corn we had scattered for them.

In the evening the man

made a fire in the fire pit in the back yard. We would stay outside listening to the radio, tending the fire until it grew dark. My life was good. The man talked to me and I understood what he wanted and I did it. I knew that I never wanted to be kicked or shot at again! This man was my friend!

I also knew how to teach the man and lady what I wanted. If I wanted one of the delicious dog cookies they kept in a jar under the sink for me I asked to be let outside. I did this by standing by the kitchen doorway. Then I went around the corner of the house, waited a minute and then barked to be let back in the house. The lady always let me in and told me I was a good boy. She gave me a cookie! People are easy to train if you have patience! I also knew that on top of the refrigerator in a metal can they kept windmill cookies. I love windmill cookies! I could hear them open that can of windmill cookies even late at night when I was sound asleep on my bed. As soon as I heard that tin top leave the can I went and sat in the doorway to the kitchen. They always shared their cookies with me, laughing guiltily at being caught raiding the cookie can in the middle of the night.

Over the years the couple

had visits from lots of kids. I love kids! I love to lick their faces because they taste so sweet. These kids were called grandchildren, yours and mine. I could always tell when they were coming for a visit. The lady carried in big bags of good smelling food. The man oiled and gassed his lawn tractors. He got his little cart ready to pull. He gave rides to the little kids and taught the bigger ones how to drive. He always said it was good training for when they needed to drive cars. The couple got excited when the kids came to visit! I could feel it! When the kids went home, the man and lady slept a lot. So did I!

One of the kids who came for a week every summer was a boy named Ryan. When he visited, Ryan and the man played baseball. Every day they played! They pitched and batted. They ran and laughed. They argued about the rules and who had the most points. But it was always just the two of them. They made up a game because they had no fielder. One threw the ball and the other batted. Then they changed sides. One day I started to chase the ball and then there were three players! I could really run fast and get the ball. If the ball went under the electric fence I could just scoot under and get it. It made for a much better game. Sometimes I ran away with the ball just for the fun of it! The man and the boy chased me yelling and laughing! It was a great trick!

The lady started to talk to the man about taking me with them when they went camping. I knew they went away sometimes. They took me to the kennel. I hated the kennel! I was lonely for the man while I was there.

It was too noisy to sleep. There were no windmill cookies! The man said no dog should go camping; they were too noisy and bothered others. Finally, the lady convinced the man to let me try. They hooked up their little camping trailer and away we went. I rode on the back seat of the truck and slept or looked out the window. I did not know what camping was but I just knew it had to be better than the kennel! I was

very quiet in the campground.
I stayed right with the man.
I did not bark even when I
heard other dogs barking. I
got to be such a good camper
the couple took me lots of
places. We went to the ocean,
the mountains and the desert.
I swam in the ocean; it was
cold and tasted like salt! I
learned to love to go camping
with them. We went lots of
places in that little camper.
We hiked and fished! They
rode their bicycles while I ran

alongside. We had great fun! It was wonderful not to have to stay behind!

The years have passed since the man picked me up at the side of the road that cold winter night. The man and I still walk every day but we are both slower! Now when I get up off of my bed in the morning my hip is stiff and it hurts. When the man gets up off of his bed he says, "Ouch, ouch." He is bent over too.

The lady is gone. The man said she died. He cried.

The man says I am his best friend and we keep each other company.

All the grandchildren who came to visit and whose faces I licked have grown up. They don't come very often anymore. " They have their own lives to lead," the man said.

Some nights in the deep of winter when the snow falls and the wind howls I remember how the man rescued me. I am warmed by the kindness of the man for a poor abused pup. The man says it was his lucky day when he found me! I think we were both lucky on that bitter cold day all those long years ago.

The End

Iris Revesz Rodak

Iris Revesz Rodak

Iris and Lee live with their wonderful dog, Joe on a small farm in Southwest Michigan. This is her second book. The first book "Annie Always" is recollections from her childhood in a small town.

To order other books by
Iris Revesz Rodak

Website Iris Rodak.com
1-800-766-1485

Printed in the United States
1462600001B/61-84